R0083435677

08/2015

Dear Parent:
Your child's love of reading starts here!

Every child learns to read in a different way and at his or her own speed. You can help your young reader improve and become more confident by encouraging his or her own interests and abilities. You can also guide your child's spiritual development by reading stories with biblical values and Bible stories, like I Can Read! books published by Zonderkidz. From books your child reads with you to the first books he or she reads alone, there are I Can Read! books for every stage of reading:

SHARED READING
Basic language, word repetition, and whimsical illustrations, ideal for sharing with your emergent reader.

BEGINNING READING
Short sentences, familiar words, and simple concepts for children eager to read on their own.

READING WITH HELP
Engaging stories, longer sentences, and language play for developing readers.

READING ALONE
Complex plots, challenging vocabulary, and high-interest topics for the independent reader.

ADVANCED READING
Short paragraphs, chapters, and exciting themes for the perfect bridge to chapter books.

I Can Read! books have introduced children to the joy of reading since 1957. Featuring award-winning authors and illustrators and a fabulous cast of beloved characters, I Can Read! books set the standard for beginning readers.

A lifetime of discovery begins with the magical words "I Can Read!"

Visit www.icanread.com for information on enriching your child's reading experience.
Visit www.zonderkidz.com for more Zonderkidz I Can Read! titles.

If you really want to become wise, you must begin
by having respect for the Lord. All those who
follow his rules have good understanding.
—*Psalm 16:1*

www.zonderkidz.com

Super Ace and the Space Traffic Jam
Text copyright © 2009 by Cheryl Crouch
Illustrations copyright © 2009 by Matt Vander Pol

Requests for information should be addressed to:
Zonderkidz, *Grand Rapids, Michigan 49530*

Library of Congress Cataloging-in-Publication Data

Crouch, Cheryl, 1968-
    Super Ace and the space traffic jam / story by Cheryl Crouch ; pictures by Matt Vander Pol.
       p. cm. -- (I can read! Level 2)
      ISBN 978-0-310-71698-3 (softcover)
       [1. Superheroes--Fiction. 2. Christian life--Fiction.] I. Vander Pol, Matt, 1972- ill. II. Title.
    PZ7.C8838Ss 2009
    [E]--dc22
                                       2008038654

Art Direction & Design: Jody Langley

Printed in China

09 10 11 12 • 4 3 2

Super Ace and the Space Traffic Jam

story by Cheryl Crouch

pictures by Matt Vander Pol

Super Ace and Sidekick Ned flew through deep, dark space.

BEEP! BEEP! BEEP!

"It's my super phone.

Someone on Planet Joop needs me!"

said Super Ace.

Super Ace and Ned raced to Joop,
but traffic stopped them.
Spaceships crowded the sky.

"I am stuck in a space traffic jam!"

Super Ace said.

"Planet Joop needs my help,

but I cannot get there."

Just then, a spaceship slammed
into another spaceship.

Crash! Boom!

The traffic jam got worse.

Sidekick Ned said,

"I wonder if this traffic jam

is the reason Planet Joop needs us."

"We don't have time to wonder.

We have to get past this traffic

to Planet Joop," said Super Ace.

Super Ace made fists.

"I am Super Ace," he said.

"I have two superpowers.

I am super strong,

and I am good looking."

Ned said, "That is true."

"I will use one of my superpowers
to make this traffic go away,"
said Super Ace.

"Which superpower?" asked Ned.

"My good looks will not help,"
Super Ace said.

"When people see my good looks,
they stop and stare at me."

Sidekick Ned said, "I can see
that your looks will not help."

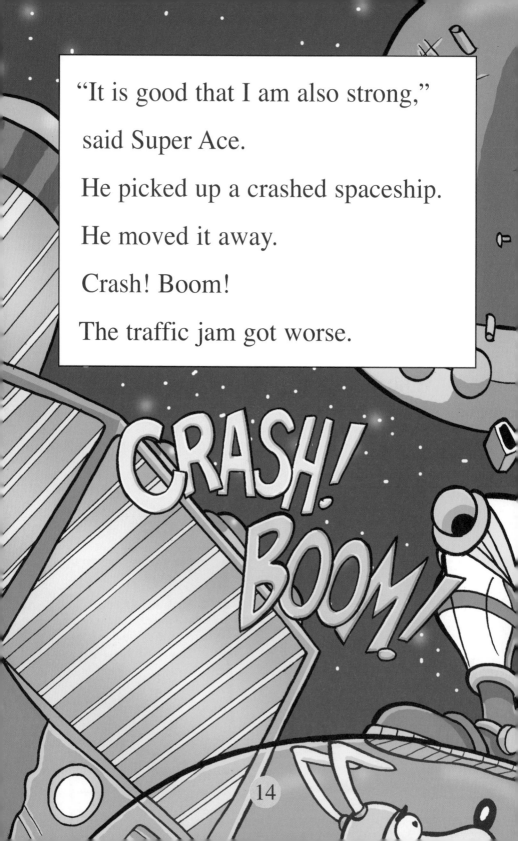

"It is good that I am also strong," said Super Ace.

He picked up a crashed spaceship.

He moved it away.

Crash! Boom!

The traffic jam got worse.

Super Ace shook his head.

"What bad drivers!

I'll try again."

He picked up another spaceship.

Sidekick Ned said, "Wait! Look!"

"The space traffic light
is broken," Ned said.

"That is sad," said Super Ace.

"But I do not have time for lights.

Planet Joop needs me."

Super Ace raised the ship high.

"Wait!" said Sidekick Ned.

"If the light is broken,

drivers do not know when to go

and when to stop.

Drivers need rules to be safe."

Super Ace let go of the ship. "But I cannot fix a traffic light with my looks or my strong arms. We are stuck, like everyone else."

Ned said, "God gave me wisdom.

God can help me solve this problem."

"I don't think wisdom is as good
as my superpowers,"
said Super Ace.
"But if you fix the light,
I can get to Planet Joop.
Then I can help them."
Sidekick Ned said, "Okay."

Ned zoomed by the stuck spaceships.

He flew to the space traffic light.

It needed new wire.

Ned had wire in his super pack.

He wired it on.

After Sidekick Ned fixed the light,
traffic started to go again.
The spaceships did not crash.

The drivers knew when to go
and when to stop.

"Great!" said Super Ace.

"Now we can get to Planet Joop."

Jooper met them on Planet Joop.

Super Ace smiled and said,

"I am here! How can I help, Jooper?"

"You already did," said Jooper.

"You both fixed our space traffic jam.

Thank you!"

Super Ace looked surprised.

"Oh," he said. "We are glad we helped.

And now, we must go help others."

Then Super Ace and Sidekick Ned
flew back into deep, dark space.